THE FLYING LIGHT

YUANHAO YANG

ONE DULL MORNING...

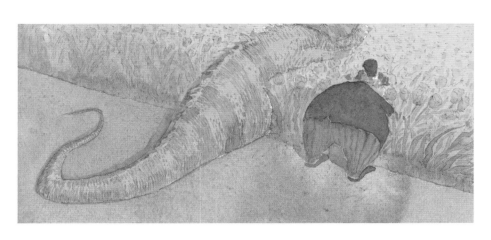

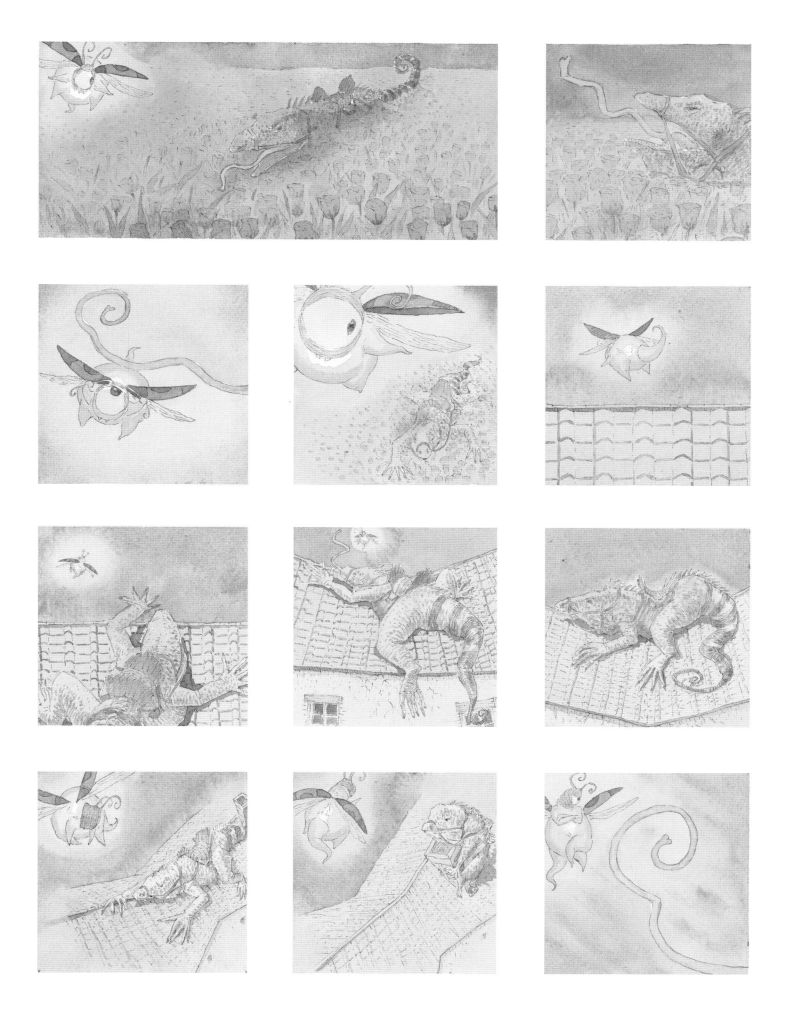

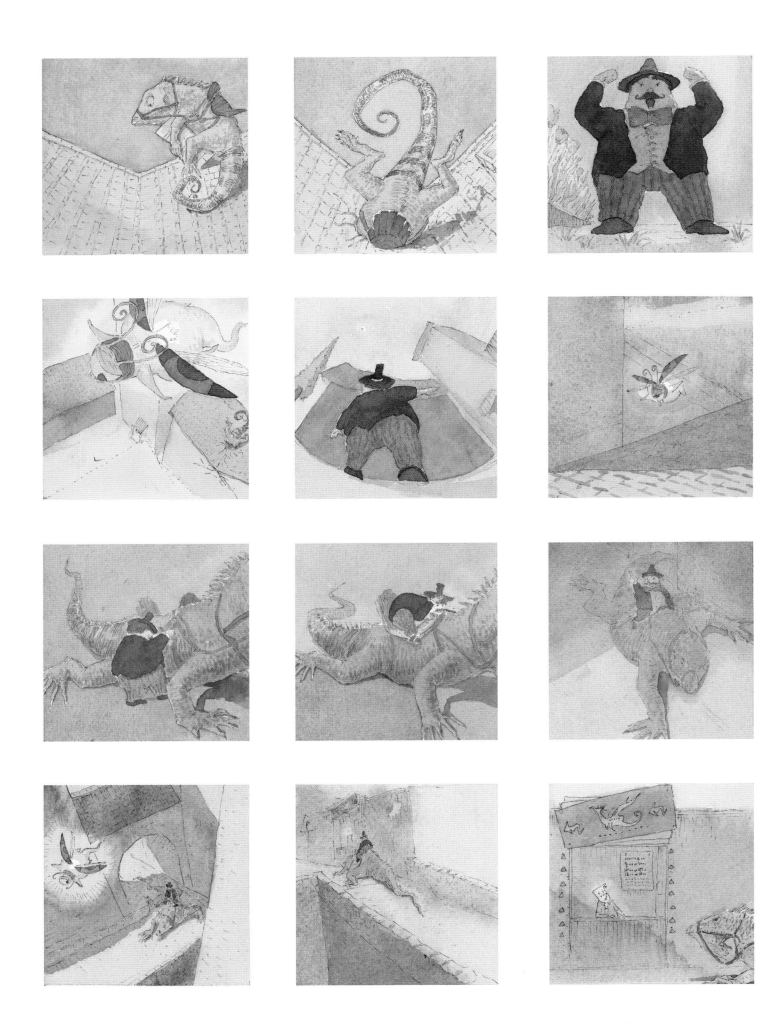

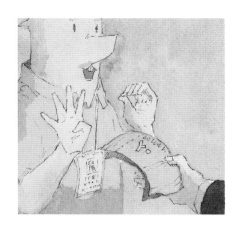

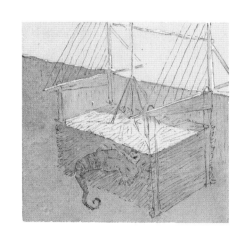

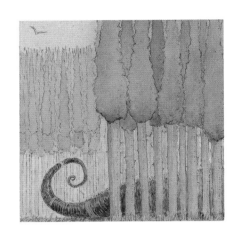

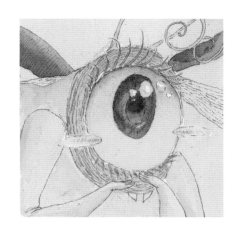

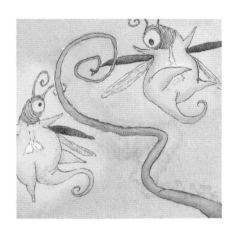

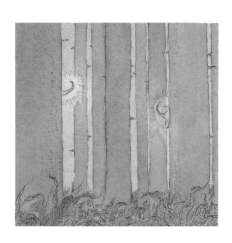

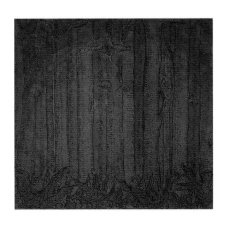

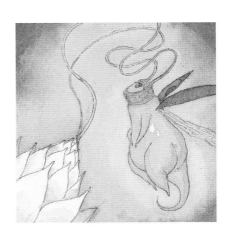

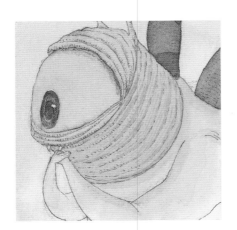

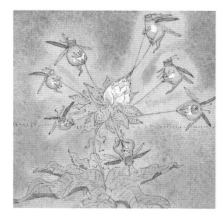
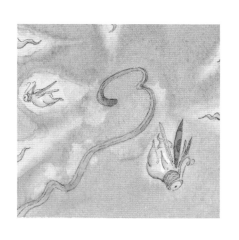
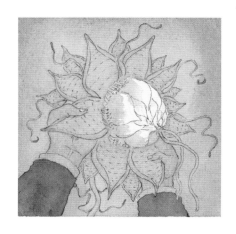

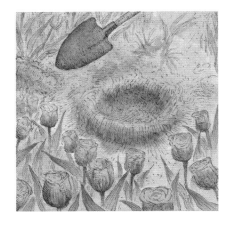

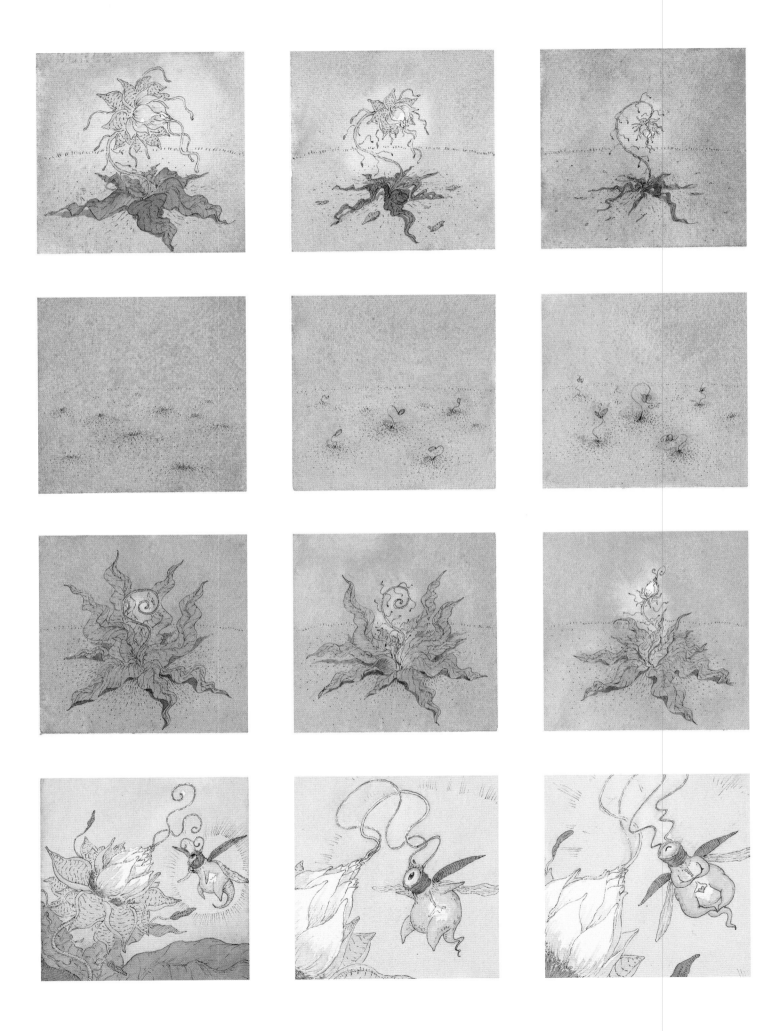

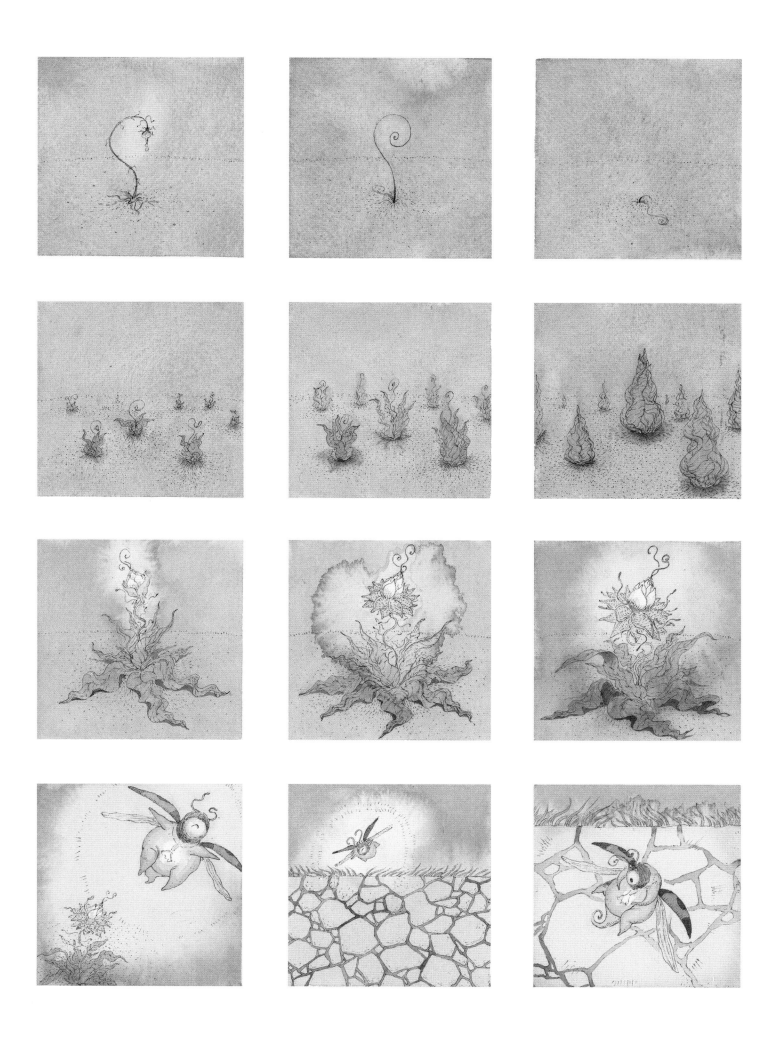

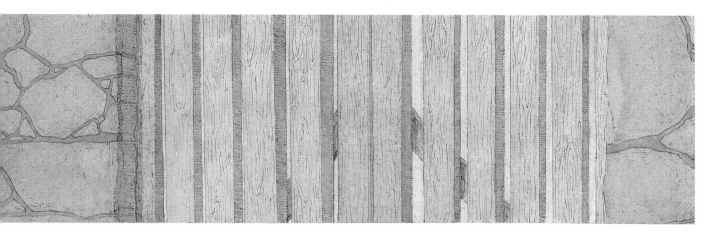

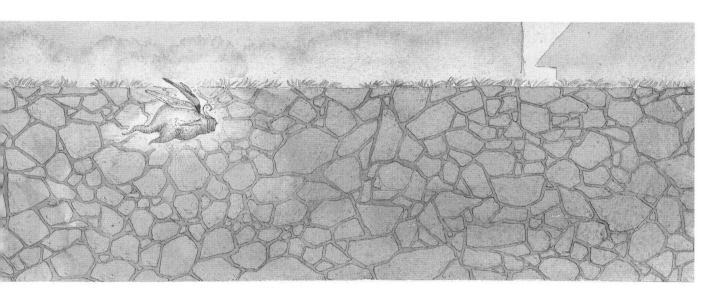

ONE BRIGHT MORNING...

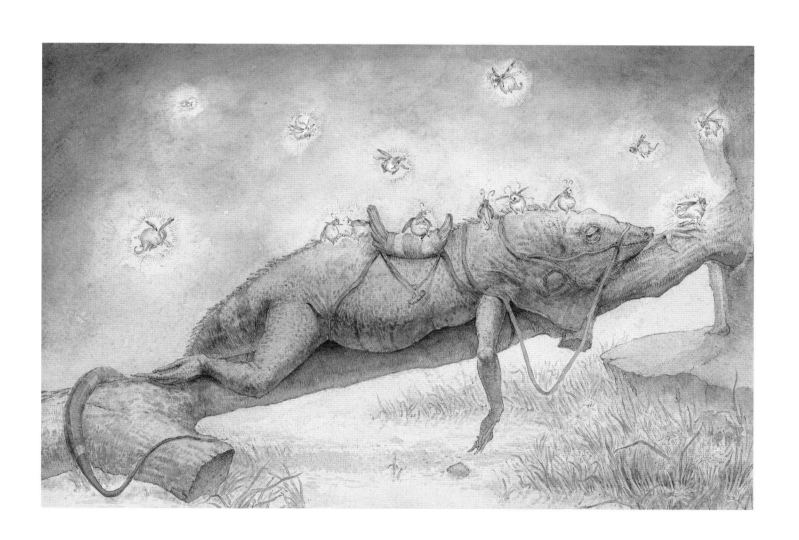

After an enchanting discovery in their
garden, a man and his giant pet lizard chase
a luminous flying creature through town
and into the forest, where they realise the
creature is also searching for something:
a flower that can replenish its light. Eager
to draw the glowing creature back to town,
the man cleverly brings back the flower
and plants it. These special flowers bloom
throughout his garden, soon drawing a flock
of luminous creatures and brightening up a
town previously cloaked in darkness.

THE FLYING LIGHT

Sincere thanks to Elyse Williams for her creative efforts in preparing this
edition for publication.

Yuanhao Yang graduated from the Department of Illustration at Nanjing
University of the Arts and now resides in Nanjing, China, where he illustrates
children's books. It is his belief that everyone views the world differently, and
he enjoys transforming these worlds into interesting forms using pen and
paper. Yuanhao likes drawing elves, as well as his dog.

 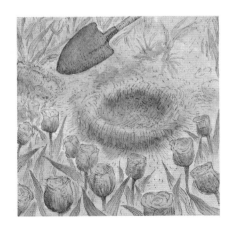